U0022208

英語 聽 & 說

初級篇

白野伊津夫
Lisa A. Stefani　　著
沈薇　譯

CD BOOK

LISTENING & SPEAKING STRATEGIES ELEMENTARY COURSE

三民書局

Original material: Copyright© Itsuo Shirono and Lisa A. Stefani, 2001
Chinese translation copyright© 2003 by San Min Book Co., Ltd.
"This translation of *Listening and Speaking Strategies – elementary course*
originally published in Japanese in 2001 is published
by arrangement with Kenkyusha Limited."

前　言

　　正如本系列書第一冊「入門篇」的前言所述，世界上有許多劃時代的大事及偉大的發明是「逆向思考」所帶來的成果。在人類普遍認為唯有燃燒東西、利用氧才能使煤油燈產生光的時代，發明大王愛迪生反其道而行，發明了電燈泡，即不需利用氧氣而製造了光。在今日防止地球繼續溫暖化的聲浪中，也正有依「逆向思考」試圖改換新的能源提供方式。例如：水可以電氣分解成氧和氫兩種化學元素，人類「逆向思考」後，希望可利用氧和氫化合成水的過程中，提煉電出來。未來，這種環保能源或許會為後代子孫帶來舒適又安全的生活。

　　《英語聽＆說》這一系列書即是依據「逆向思考」的理念所企劃出來的語言學習書。本「初級篇」是此系列書的第二冊，主要是以學完「入門篇」的學習者為對象編輯而成。第一冊已敘述過逆向思考在英語會話學習上的重要性，在此再稍做說明。我們之所以學習外語，是為了能夠流利地與外國人溝通，而傳統的英語學習方式也理所當然是以教「說英語」開始。不過，即使有為數眾多的人按照傳統的英語學習方式學習，也只有少數人能自由地以英語與人暢談。為了突破這種英語學習的瓶頸，本系列書特地引薦「聽英語」的學習法，期待能讓學習者盡快以流利的英語與人溝通。

　　從「聽」到「說」本來就是人類學習語言的自然過程。試想，若沒有母親在身邊長期不斷地說話引導，小孩根本無從學會說話。小孩原本不會說一宁　語，是先默默聽母親所講的話，在約略懂得母親話裡的涵義之後，才不斷試著模仿說出。經過這樣的反覆練習後，小孩開始能流利地與大人溝通。我們即依據上述兒

童學習語言的過程完成此系列書，各章皆由從「聽」(Listening)開始再到「說」(Speaking) 的結構組成。

經常可以聽到學習者抱怨：「能開口說一些些英語，但在聽的方面就是不行」，這就是傳統教學上注重「從說開始」的弊病。由於不懂對方在說什麼，所以內心感到強烈的不安與害怕，不僅無法與外國人自在地聊天，相反地，還受到相當大的挫折而痛苦不已。遇到這種瓶頸後，根本再也無法提高英語會話能力了。若是我們改變學習方式，「從聽開始」學習英語，相信不久即能聽懂外國人說的話，可以消除向來的不安與恐懼，愉悅地與他們對談，在往後的英語會話上也必定有很大的進步。

「從聽開始」學習的好處還不只這些。當我們的聽力提升之後，即能隨意捕捉身邊所聽到的英語，進而理解其涵義，如電視和廣播的外國新聞以及英語節目等，這些英語資訊正大量地「輸入」(input) 到我們的腦海中，經儲存、吸收後，即可融合成自己的意見及感想，依不同的會話場景「輸出」(output) 出去。達到這個階段後，即能隨時與外國人暢所欲言，相信外國人士也會期待下一次與你的愉快對話。

在經濟及其他事物都已全球化進展的今日世界，英語早就是世界性的共通語言，是地球村所有人的最佳溝通利器。衷心希望依逆向思考理念製作完成的此系列書能幫助各位精進英語會話能力，並在商場上無往不利，進而幫助世界公民理解彼此之間文化及語言上的差異。

白野伊津夫
Lisa A. Stefani

目 次

前言
本書使用方法

本書使用方法

本書共十章，各章分 Listening 及 Speaking 兩大部分，兩個部分再各由三個小單元組成。

Listening

首先出現的「Warm-up/Pre-questions」是測驗第一次聽完會話內容後的理解程度的選擇題，請聽完 CD 播放一次後立即作答。只要掌握會話的大概內容，得到正確的答案即可，不需在意細節或刻意熟習每個字句。由於是聽力的熱身運動，所以可以輕鬆面對。

「聽力技巧」中會介紹有益於提升理解力的聽力秘訣。為求實際聽懂多種場景下的英語會話，除了掌握發音的基本原則外，也必須擁有具實戰力的聽力技巧。例如數字，並不需要將英文數字一個一個置換成中文理解，而是應該掌握用英語瞭解英文數字意義的訣竅。這個單元即說明實用的聽力技巧，並且提供練習題幫助熟練。

「Listening Quiz」是驗收成果測驗。在了解英語的發音、提升聽力之後，再聽一次會話，測驗能正確聽懂多少的會話內容。請利用之前學習的聽力技巧聆聽，相信可以 100% 理解。無法正確回答時，請務必反覆聽 CD 直到徹底了解為止。

Speaking

一開始的「會話」(dialog) 可說是該章的重點，介紹並說明該章的主題內容。首先，請先默念該會話內容理解意思，若有不懂的地方再看「中譯」或「關鍵字」說明。接下來聽 CD，充分掌握英語的發音、節奏及語調後再發出聲音朗讀。朗讀時，最好是將自己融入為會話主角，並確認自己的英語是否與 CD 播放的英語一樣流暢。建議可以採取聽 CD 後朗誦、朗誦後聽 CD 的間歇式 (interval) 練習法學習。若對發音有自信，也可以採用投影練習法 (shadow training)，這是緊

跟著 CD 馬上覆誦的有效學習法。請確實跟隨 CD 自行朗誦，看看自己的發音是否接近外國人的母語。經過這一連串的練習，至少可誦唸 20 到 30 次的會話，相信必能幫助學習者脫口說出自然流利的英語。

「說法（代換、角色扮演）」中介紹並解說各章會話主題的基本及重要的語句表達方式，熟記以及活用這些語句將可大幅提升會話實力。首先請檢測是否了解英語語句的意義，再看「解說」釐清概念，也可以一併記下其他的相關語句。接下來仔細聽 CD 做「代換、角色扮演」的練習。「代換」練習是邊看基本句邊聽 CD 的代換詞句部分，再覆誦整句話，之後聆聽 CD 播放完整代換句的正確發音，請反覆練習直到可以說出流暢的英語句子來。「角色扮演」是視 CD 為談話對象的練習，先注意聆聽完整的對話示範，然後當聽到嗶一聲後說出適切的英語對應。剛開始可以看書說，但希望經過幾次練習後能不用看書而立即回答。

「實力測驗」是提供某一情境，讓學習者自我檢驗是否能就所學說出流利的英語對應。目的並非要求「正確的回答」，而是能以輕鬆的態度立刻說出自己想表達的話，讓對方了解，即使是稍微不正確的英語也無妨。最後會提供一個參考解答。

Weather 天 氣

Listening

Warm-up / Pre-questions

請聽《Track 1》的會話後回答下面問題。

南加州今天的氣溫是幾度？
- (A) 華氏 12 度
- (B) 華氏 35 度
- (C) 華氏 50 度

解答	(C)

聽力技巧

1. 聽懂數字 (1)……數值、數量（正數）

英語的正數唸法如下：

123 = one hundred and twenty-three

1,234 = one thousand, two hundred and thirty-four

1,234,567 = one million, two hundred, thirty-four thousand, five hundred and sixty-seven

請留意下列數字在發音上的不同：

13 [θɝ`tin] vs. 30 [`θɝtɪ] / 14 [for`tin] vs. 40 [`fɔrtɪ] /
15 [fɪf`tin] vs. 50 [`fɪftɪ] / 16 [sɪks`tin] vs. 60 [`sɪkstɪ] /
17 [ˌsɛvən`tin] vs. 70 [`sɛvəntɪ] / 18 [e`tɪn] vs. 80 [`etɪ] /
19 [naɪn`tin] vs. 90 [`naɪntɪ]

數字 13 到 19 中最後 -teen 的部分須加強且拉長發音。

練習 1

◎ 請聽《Track 2》並在括弧內填入正確數字。

1. Temperatures, a high of (   ), and a low of (   ) degrees.

2. The hurricane is expected to bring (   ) mm to (   ) mm of rain to Miami.

3. Heavy rain destroyed (   ) structures, flooded about (   ) houses, and caused landslides in (   ) places.

> 解答　1. Temperatures, a high of (90), and a low of (80) degrees.
>
> 2. The hurricane is expected to bring (200) mm to (300) mm of rain to Miami.
>
> 3. Heavy rain destroyed (56) structures, flooded about (14,000) houses, and caused landslides in (130) places.

2. 聽懂數字 (2)……數值、數量（小數、分數）

英語的小數與分數唸法如下：

0.4 = (zero) point four　　0.56 =(zero) point five six

1/2 = a half　　1/3 = a third *or* one-third　　2/3 = two-thirds

1/4 = a quarter *or* a fourth *or* one-fourth

3 4/5 = three and four-fifths

練習 2

◎ 請聽《Track 3》並在括弧內填入正確數字。

1. The magnitude of the earthquake was (   ) on the Richter scale.

2. The report says (   ) million homes were sold last year.

3. About (　　) of women in the world cannot read nor write.

解答　1. The magnitude of the earthquake was (4.6) on the Richter scale.
2. The report says (2.73) million homes were sold last year.
3. About (2/3) of women in the world cannot read nor write.

Listening Quiz

 請聽《Track 1》的會話後回答下面問題。

芝加哥的積雪多達幾英吋?

(A) 5 英吋

(B) 12 英吋

(C) 35 英吋

(D) 50 英吋

解答　　　　　　　　　　　　　　　　　　　　　(B)

Speaking

會話

 請再聽一次《Track 1》。

A: Good morning, Ellen. My goodness, it's really cold in this office!

B: I know, Janice. I turned the heat on this morning when I got to work but it is still cold in here.

A: I can't believe this weather! 50 degrees in Southern California!

B: It's incredible. Last night it got down to 35 degrees!

A: That is just too cold for me. I moved here because I like warm weather!

B: Oh, Janice, we shouldn't complain. Think about those people living in Chicago. They are having a blizzard and 12 inches of snow now.

A: I suppose you're right. But still, this is really cold weather for our location.

B: I think so too and the weather forecast is calling for more of the same for the rest of the week.

A: You must be kidding!

中譯

A: 早安，愛倫。我的老天，辦公室可真是夠冷的!

B: 是啊，珍妮絲。我一早來上班就已經先把暖氣打開了，不過還是很冷。

A: 真不敢相信會是這種天氣，在南加州竟然有到 50 度!

B：的確不可思議。昨晚甚至還降到 35 度呢。

A：我搬到這兒來就是因為我喜歡溫暖的氣候,可是這樣的天氣對我來說太冷了。

B：唉,珍妮絲,其實我們不該再抱怨了。想想那些住在芝加哥的人,現在不但遭暴風雪來襲,甚至連積雪也已經高達12英吋了。

A：我想妳說得也對,不過我還是認為這樣的天氣對這裡來說實在是太冷了。

B：我也這麼認為,不過天氣預報說,這個禮拜接下來都將會是這種天氣。

A：妳不是在開玩笑吧?!

關鍵字

My goodness!　哎呀! 我的天呀! (有驚訝、不可置信之意,屬於誇張的口語用法)

50 degrees　(此處指) 華氏 50 度 (相當於攝氏 10 度)

incredible　令人難以置信的

complain　抱怨,訴苦

blizzard　暴風雪

for our location　以我們所在的地點而言

calling for　預報

You must be kidding!　你一定在開玩笑吧! (表不敢置信; 美國口語常見的用法)

天氣的說法

 請聽《Track 4》。

---

1. A: It's a beautiful day, isn't it?

   B: It sure is.

2. A: It's very hot and muggy today, isn't it?

   B: Yes, it's very miserable.

3. A: It looks like rain, doesn't it?

   B: Yes, you'd better take an umbrella with you.

解說

● 當我們要用英語說「天氣真好」或「天氣很炎熱」的句子時，可以用 it 造基本句，如 It's a beautiful day, isn't it? 或 It's very hot today, isn't it?，有時也可以省略 It's，說成 Very hot today, isn't it?。另外，通常會用 Yes, it is. / Yes, it sure/certainly is. / Yes, isn't it? 等來回應與天氣有關的問候語。

● 看到天空烏雲密佈、似乎要下雨時，可以用 it looks like 敘述，說成 It looks like rain, doesn't it?（好像要下雨了）。若要表示預見情況不甚樂觀時，可用 I'm afraid 修飾，即說成 I'm afraid it's going to rain this afternoon.（今天下午恐怕會下雨）。

練習 1【代換】

請隨《Track 5》做代換練習。

1. It's a beautiful day, isn't it?

   an awful day, isn't it?
   hot and muggy today, isn't it?
   very cold today, isn't it?
   rather chilly today, isn't it?

2. It looks like rain, doesn't it?

rain any minute, doesn't it?

rain this afternoon, doesn't it?

snow tonight, doesn't it?

it's going to clear up, doesn't it?

練習 2【角色扮演】

 請隨《Track 6》在嗶一聲後唸出灰色部分的句子。

1. A: It's a lovely day, isn't it?

B: It sure is.

2. A: It's very cold outside, isn't it?

B: Yes, it's freezing.

3. A: What an awful day!

B: Yes, it's dreadfully wet and windy.

實力測驗

今天的天氣很悶熱。你出外辦事時，巧遇外國朋友 Jack，這時你
會如何用英語和他打招呼，並且談到與天氣有關的話題呢？

參考解答　Hi, Jack. What nasty weather we're having! It's so
hot and muggy.

<table>
<tr><td>Chapter
2</td><td>**At the Post Office**</td><td>在郵局</td></tr>
</table>

Listening

Warm-up / Pre-questions

 請聽《Track 7》的會話後回答下面問題。

這位女士想要寄信，她會用什麼郵寄方式寄到日本呢？

(A) 一般平信

(B) 航空

(C) 快捷

解答　　　　　　　　　　　　　　　　　　　　　　　　　(C)

聽力技巧

1. 聽懂數字 (3)⋯⋯日期

英語的重要日期唸法如下：

2001年 = two thousand one / 9月15日 September fifteenth *or* the fifteenth of September

1日 = first / 2日 = second / 3日 = third / 4日 = fourth / 5日 = fifth / 6日 = sixth / 7日 = seventh / 8日 = eighth / 9日 = ninth / 10日 = tenth / 11日 = eleventh / 12日 / = twelfth / 13日 = thirteenth / 21日 = twenty-first / 22日 = twenty-second / 23日 = twenty-third

September 10 – October 5 = September tenth to October fifth

Monday – Friday = Monday to Friday *or* Monday through Friday

練習 1

 請聽《Track 8》並在括弧內填入正確答案。

1. It will take about (   ) weeks for the letter to get to Japan if you send it by surface mail.

2. The package should arrive there by July (   ).

3. It will arrive in (   ) to (   ) working days.

> 解答　1. It will take about (3) weeks for the letter to get to Japan if you send it by surface mail.
> 2. The package should arrive there by July (15th).
> 3. It will arrive in (2) to (3) working days.

2. 聽懂數字 (4)……時間、金錢、電話號碼

英語的時間唸法如下：

上午8點 = eight (o'clock) in the morning *or* eight a.m.

正午 = (twelve) noon / 下午3點 = three (o'clock) in the afternoon

午夜12點 = (twelve o'clock) midnight

9點15分 = nine fifteen, *or* fifteen (minutes) past nine, *or* a quarter past nine

差10分6點 = ten to six, *or* ten minutes before six

英語的金錢唸法如下：

$78.35 = seventy-eight dollars 35 cents *or* seventy-eight thirty-five

唸電話號碼時，是一個一個唸出數字的音，其中 0 有 zero [ˋzɪro] 或 o [o] 兩種唸法。

03-3456-7809 = o[o] (*or* zero), three, three, four, five, six, seven, eight, o [o] (*or* zero), nine

練習 2

請聽《Track 9》並在括弧內填入正確數字。

1. We are open from (　　　) a.m. to (　　　) p.m. Monday through Friday.

2. That'll be (　　　) dollars and (　　　) cents.

3. My phone number is (　　　　　　).

解答　1. We are open from (9) a.m. to (6) p.m. Monday through Friday.

2. That'll be (114) dollars and (50) cents.

3. My phone number is (323-402-7586).

Listening Quiz

請聽《Track 7》的會話後回答下面問題。

寄這封信的郵資是多少錢？

(A) 3 dollars.

(B) 4 dollars.

(C) 8 dollars and 95 cents.

(D) 9 dollars and 85 cents.

解答　　　　　　　　　　　　　　　　　　　　　　　(D)

Speaking

會話

 請再聽一次《Track 7》。

A: Hi. How can I help you?

B: I'd like to send this letter to Japan.

A: By airmail or surface mail?

B: I think I would like to send it by airmail. How long does that take?

A: About a week.

B: About a week? That is too long. Is there a way I can get it to Japan faster?

A: Sure there is. If you send it by Priority mail, it will arrive in 3–4 working days.

B: That's better. How much does it cost?

A: It depends on the weight. Let me weigh your letter. Well, your letter will cost $9.85.

B: That's not bad at all. I will send it Priority mail.

A: Okay then, you need to fill out this Priority envelope and put your letter in it. That will be $9.85, please.

中譯

A: 妳好，有什麼可以為妳服務的嗎?

B: 我想寄信到日本。

A: 請問要寄航空還是水陸?

B: 寄航空好了。大約需要多久時間?

A: 大約一個禮拜。

B: 大約一個禮拜? 太慢了。還有沒有更快寄到日本的方式?

A: 當然有。假如妳選寄快捷,大約只需要三到四個工作天便可寄達。

B: 這種比較好。請問要多少錢?

A: 要看信件的重量。先讓我來秤秤看妳的信。嗯,這封信的郵資是 9 塊 85 分美元。

B: 也不算貴,我就寄快捷。

A: 好的,那麼請妳填好快捷信封上的資料,再將信放進去。最後請付 9 塊 85 分。

關鍵字

surface mail 一般平信,水陸路郵件(相對於 airmail 而言)

Priority mail 優先處理的郵件(限時專送的一種,在此譯為快捷)

working day 工作天(不包含假日)

depend on 根據,依~為準

weigh 秤重

fill out 填寫(文件表格)

郵寄的說法

 請聽《Track 10》。

1. A: I'd like to send this letter to Japan by airmail.
   B: All right. That'll be 2 dollars and 60 cents.

2. A: How much does it cost if I send this package to Japan by airmail?

B: 25 dollars and 40 cents. Please fill out this customs declaration form.

3. A: I'd like to have ten 50 cent stamps.

B: All right. Here you are.

解說

● 在外國郵局表達「我想要寄信」時，可以使用比較禮貌的 I'd like to 的句型，說成如 I'd like to send this letter to Japan. 的句子。另外，by airmail 是「寄航空」的意思，「寄水陸／一般平信」的英文則是 by ship 或 by surface mail。

● 「明信片」的英文是 postcard，「風景明信片」是 picture postcard；「郵票」是 stamp，也可以說成 postage stamp。「郵資」則是 postage，當要詢問郵資是多少錢時，可說 How much does it cost...? 或 What is the postage of this parcel? 另外，寄包裹到國外時，記得必須填寫 customs declaration form（海關申報單）上面的必要事項。

練習 1【代換】

 請隨《Track 11》做代換練習。

1. I'd like to send this letter to Japan by airmail.

> send this picture postcard to Japan by airmail.
> send this package to Japan by ship.
> have five 50 cent stamps.
> insure this parcel.

2. How much does it cost if I send this letter to Japan by airmail?

I send this picture postcard to Japan by airmail?
I send this package to Japan by ship?
I send this document by express?
I insure this parcel?

練習 2【角色扮演】

 請隨《Track 12》在嗶一聲後唸出灰色部分的句子。

1. A: I'd like to send this package to Japan.

   B: By airmail or surface mail?

2. A: How long will it take for the letter to get to Japan if I send it by airmail?

   B: About a week.

3. A: How much does it cost if I send this letter by express?

   B: 8 dollars and 50 cents.

實力測驗

你想用船運寄一件包裹到台灣，包裹裡頭裝有一些書，這時該如何開口跟外國郵局的人說明呢？

參考解答 I'd like to send this parcel of books to Taiwan by ship.

Business Travel 出　差

Listening

Warm-up / Pre-questions

請聽《Track 13》的會話後回答下面問題。

這段會話的場景是在哪裡?

(A) 長途巴士裡

(B) 飛機上

(C) 電車裡

解答　　　　　　　　　　　　　　　　　　　　　　(B)

聽力技巧

1. 聽懂專有名詞 ⑴……人名

要聽懂英語會話裡的人名一向不是件容易的事,我們通常可以抓住外國人名字(first name)的音,但較難記下外國人的姓(last name)。這是由於外國人的名字多取自聖經上所出現的人名,而這些人名是我們所熟悉的;另外是由於英美人士、特別是由多種民族組成的美國人多半沿用祖先的姓的緣故。要聽懂外國人名,建議先從熟悉 first name 開始。

常見的男性 first name:

Adam / Bill / Chris / David / Edward / Frank / George / Harry / Ian / John / Kevin / Luke / Mark / Neil / Oliver / Paul / Richard / Steve / Tom / Vincent / Walter

常見的女性 first name:

Anne / Barbara / Carol / Diane / Elizabeth / Faith / Gloria / Helen / Irene / Jane / Katherine / Lisa / Mary / Nancy / Olivia / Patricia / Ruth / Susan / Teresa / Vivian / Wendy

last name 的例子：

Anderson / Benson / Carlson / Davis / Eisenberg / Fischer / Glenn / Howel / Irwin / Jackson / Keaten / Lee / McNeal / Newcomb / Owen / Palmer / Robinson / Stewart / Turner / Updike / Valentine / Watson / Young / Zimmerman

練習 1

 請聽《Track 14》並在括弧內填入人名。

1. Hi. My name is (　　　　).
2. Excuse me. I'd like to see Ms. (　　　　), please.
3. (　　　　), there was a call from (　　　　) a minute ago.

解答　1. Hi. My name is (John Anderson).
　　　2. Excuse me. I'd like to see Ms. (Diane Stewart), please.
　　　3. (Barbara), there was a call from (Mark Eliot) a minute ago.

2. 聽懂專有名詞 (2)……公司名

公司名和人名一樣複雜，命名也多樣化，但後面通常還會加上 Co. Corp. Inc. Ltd. 等字，這些分別是 company, corporation（[股份]有限公司）、incorporated（法人[公司]組織的）及 limited（〈公司等〉有限責任的）的縮寫。

公司名的例子：

Carlton Co. / Garrett Huber Corp. / Nicolson Inc. / A. Grantham & Son Ltd. / Wade Technologies International Inc. / JDR Enterprises Inc.

練習 2

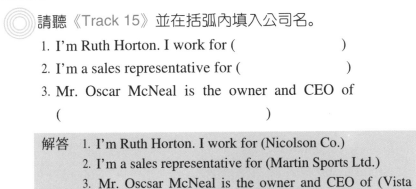

請聽《Track 15》並在括弧內填入公司名。

1. I'm Ruth Horton. I work for (   )

2. I'm a sales representative for (   )

3. Mr. Oscar McNeal is the owner and CEO of

(   )

> 解答　1. I'm Ruth Horton. I work for (Nicolson Co.)
>
> 2. I'm a sales representative for (Martin Sports Ltd.)
>
> 3. Mr. Oscsar McNeal is the owner and CEO of (Vista Technologies International Inc.)

Listening Quiz

請聽《Track 13》的會話後回答下面問題。

Allen Kirkland 先生在哪一家公司上班?

(A) Residence Medical Equipment

(B) Stanley Owen Co.

(C) Express Software International

(D) Seattle Medical Equipment

解答   (A)

Speaking

會話

 請再聽一次《Track 13》。

A: Excuse me. Are you sure you are in the right seat?

B: Let me see. Oh, excuse me! I am in the wrong seat. I should be in 23A, the window seat. Sorry.

A: No problem. Thanks for moving. My name is Stanley Owen.

B: Hi, Stanley. I'm Allen Kirkland. It's nice to meet you.

A: Nice to meet you, too. What takes you to Seattle today?

B: I am flying there on business.

A: So am I. What do you do?

B: I am a sales representative for Residence Medical Equipment. There is a big medical convention this weekend and I will be operating a display booth.

A: Great. What kind of medical equipment do you sell?

B: Mostly surgical instruments. What do you do?

A: I am a sales representative also. I work for a company called Express Software International.

B: What kind of business will you be doing in Seattle?

A: I will be meeting some of our new clients to find out their specific software needs.

B: That sounds pretty exciting.

中譯

A: 對不起，請問你確定坐對機位了嗎?

B：讓我看一下。喔，抱歉，我坐錯位置了。我的位置是 23A 靠窗的才對，真是對不起。

A：沒關係，謝謝你換位子。我是史丹利·歐文。

B：你好，史丹利。我是艾倫·科蘭，幸會。

A：幸會，請問你今天到西雅圖是為了辦什麼事？

B：我要去出差。

A：我也是。請問你的工作是？

B：我是居家醫療器材公司的業務代表。這個週末在西雅圖有舉辦一場大型的醫學會議，我將在那負責展示一個攤位。

A：很好嘛！請問你們展售的是什麼類型的醫療器材？

B：以手術醫療儀器為主。請問你是做哪一行？

A：我也是一位業務代表，我的公司是快捷軟體國際公司。

B：請問你到西雅圖的工作是什麼？

A：我會與一些新客戶會面，並了解他們對特殊軟體的需求。

B：聽起來也很有意思！

關鍵字

window seat　靠窗座位（cf. aisle seat　靠走道座位）

What takes you to Seattle today?　你到西雅圖是為了辦什麼事？（take 有「帶走」「引導」的意味。cf. What has brought you here?「你為了什麼事來這裡?」）

fly　搭飛機去

sales representative　業務代表（比 salesman 的說法正式）

convention　會議，大會

operate a display booth　負責展示攤位介紹產品

medical equipment　醫療器材

surgical instrument　手術儀器

find out　找出，發現

software　（電腦）軟體

sound　聽起來，似乎

與工作有關的說法

請聽《Track 16》。

1. A: What do you do for a living?

   B: I'm a sales representative.

2. A: Who do you work for?

   B: I work for Nicolson Company.

3. A: What department are you in?

   B: I'm in the Accounting Department.

解說

● 想知道對方的職業，可以用 What kind of work do you do? 或 What do you do for a living? 詢問，聽話者回答時只要在 I'm 之後接職業名即可，如從事旅行工作的人可以回答 I'm a travel agent.。

● 想知道對方在哪一家公司上班，可以用基本句 What company do you work for? 或 What do you work for? 來詢問，這兩句是很常用的問句；除了可以回答 I work for + 公司名之外，也可以說 I'm with + 公司名，例如：I'm with Greenwood Publishing. （我在綠木出版社工作）。

● 另外，最好也熟習外國公司部門的英文名稱。主要的部門名稱如下：

總務部	General Affairs Division
會計部	General Accounting Division
營業部	Sales Division
生產部	Production Division
國外營業部	Overseas Business Division
公關室	Public Relations Office
人事科	Personnel Department
會計科	Accounting Department
財政科	Finance Department
業務科	Sales Department
企劃科	Planning Department
品管科	Production Administration Department

練習 1 【代換】

 請隨《Track 17》做代換練習。

1. I'm a sales representative.
   a financial advisor.
   a marketing consultant.
   an engineer.
   an accountant.

2. I work for Brown Trading Co.
   United Technologies Inc.
   Jennings Controls Corp.
   Lexington Press.
   the Carlton Hotel.

練習 2【角色扮演】

 請隨《Track 18》在嗶一聲後唸出灰色部分的句子。

1. A: What kind of work do you do?

   B: I'm a real estate agent.

2. A: Who do you work for?

   B: I work for Hearst and Willams Corp.

3. A: What department are you in?

   B: I'm in the personnel department.

實力測驗

你是一位電腦製圖專業人員，在洛杉磯的 Apex Multimedia International 公司上班。有一次搭飛機到海外出差，一位坐在旁邊的旅客問你 What do you do? 時，你要如何回答呢？

參考解答　　I'm a computer graphics artist for Apex Multimedia International in Los Angeles.

Chapter 4　Taking a Vacation　休　假

≡ Listening ≡

Warm-up / Pre-questions

◎ 請聽《Track 19》的會話後回答下面問題。

這段會話裡談論的是哪個季節?

(A) 夏

(B) 秋

(C) 冬

解答　(C)

聽力技巧

1. 聽懂專有名詞 (3)……地名

會話中經常能聽到如出生地、公司所在地及出差地等等的地名,由於這些外國地名和中文譯名的發音大異其趣,所以必須留意正確唸法。

主要都市如下:

Washington D.C.(華盛頓)/ New York / San Francisco(舊金山)/ Los Angeles(洛杉磯)/ London / Paris / Berlin(柏林)/ Warsaw(華沙)/ Madrid(馬德里)/ Amsterdam(阿姆斯特丹)/ Athens(雅典)/ Canberra(坎培拉)/ Wellington(威靈頓)/ Beijing(北京)/ Seoul(漢城)

練習 1

◎ 請聽《Track 20》並在括弧內填入地名。

1. I'm from (　　　　).
2. Our company's head office is in (　　　　), the capital of (　　　　).
3. Mr. Glenn was transferred to the (　　　　) office last month.

> 解答　1. I'm from (California).
> 　　　2. Our company's head office is in (Trenton), the capital of (New Jersey).
> 　　　3. Mr. Glenn was transferred to the (Sacramento) office last month.

2. 聽懂專有名詞 (4)⋯⋯國名、機構名 （簡稱）

國名和機構名也是聽力重點。無論是到海外旅行或出差，在和外國人打開話匣子時，難免會提到國家的名稱。英語的國名也和中文譯名的發音差很多，所以也必須留意。另外，建築物及機構的名稱，由於常採用簡稱而更難完全聽懂，建議可先加強熟記主要機構的縮寫唸法。

主要國家如下：

the U.S.（美國）/ England [Britain]（英國）/ Germany（德國）/ Holland [the Netherlands]（荷蘭）/ Switzerland（瑞士）/ Australia（澳洲）/ New Zealand（紐西蘭）/ Thailand（泰國）/ Korea（韓國）/ China（中國）

主要機構的簡稱如下：

the U.N.（聯合國）/ AAA（全美汽車協會）/ UNESCO（聯合國教育科學暨文化組織）/ NASA（〈美國〉國家航空暨太空總署）/ the EU（歐洲聯盟）/ the FBI（〈美國〉聯邦調查局）/ NBA

（全美籃球協會）/ NFL（全美美式足球聯盟）/ OPEC（石油輸出國家組織）/ WHO（世界衛生組織）

練習 2

◎ 請聽《Track 21》並在括弧內填入國名、建築物名稱或機構的簡稱。

1. I've never been to (　　　　　).

2. Tickets for the June 25 show at (　　　　　　　　) will go on sale on Wednesday.

3. Mr. Horton has worked at (　　　　　) for 20 years.

> 解答　1. I've never been to (Egypt).
>
> 2. Tickets for the June 25 show at (Madison Square Garden) will go on sale on Wednesday.
>
> 3. Mr. Horton has worked at (UNESCO) for 20 years.

Listening Quiz

◎ 請聽《Track 19》的會話後回答下面問題。

Bill 的假期計劃是什麼?

(A) 到舊金山探望父母

(B) 到舊金山觀光

(C) 帶小孩到芝加哥探望父母

(D) 帶小孩到芝加哥滑雪

解答　(C)

Speaking

會話

 請再聽一次《Track 19》。

A: I am so happy that this is our last day of work and then we are closed for a week.

B: Me, too, Aaron. I can hardly wait to get a whole week off.

A: This has been a pretty stressful year, hasn't it, Bill?

B: You can say that again! With the merger and the two new big accounts, it's given me gray hair.

A: Yeah. Are you doing anything special during the time off?

B: You bet! I am taking my family back to Chicago to spend Christmas with my parents.

A: Oh. That will be fun — cold, but fun. Do you get back there often?

B: No, not really. That is one of the reasons that I want to go. I want my kids to get to know their grandparents and to get to see snow.

A: Yes. It's hard living away from your family.

B: What are you doing, Aaron?

A: I am taking my family to San Francisco to spend Hanukkah with my family.

B: Have your kids been there before?

A: Yes, we try to go once or twice a year. If I am tied up at work, my wife usually takes them.

B: That's great. Well, I hope you and your family have a happy holiday. See you next week.

A: Thanks. You, too, Bill. Enjoy the holiday with your family.

中譯

A: 我真高興今天工作結束後，就能放一個禮拜的假了！

B: 我也是，艾倫。我已經等不及要放一個禮拜的假了。

A: 這一年真是累得讓人喘不過氣來，你說是吧，比爾？

B: 這還用說！光為了忙合併以及那兩大客戶的事，就已經讓我長白頭髮了。

A: 是啊。你的假期有沒有什麼特別計畫？

B: 當然有啦！我準備帶家人返回芝加哥與父母一同歡度聖誕節。

A: 噢。那裡雖然冷，但你們應該會玩得很盡興的。你常回去嗎？

B: 不，並沒有。這也正是為什麼我想要回去的原因之一。我希望我的孩子們可以多認識祖父母，同時也讓他們看看雪。

A: 是啊，這離家鄉生活也真不是件容易的事。

B: 那麼艾倫你有什麼計畫？

A: 我要帶我的家人一起去舊金山參加猶太慶典。

B: 你的孩子之前有去過那裡嗎？

A: 有的，我們盡量一年去一次或兩次。如果我工作太忙無法脫身的話，我太太便會帶他們去。

B: 真好！那麼，祝你們一家有個愉快的假期。下個禮拜見囉！

A: 謝謝。比爾，你也一樣，好好享受和家人共聚的假期！

關鍵字

can hardly wait　迫不及待

a whole week off 一整週的休假

You can say that again! 你說得對極了！（完全贊同的強調說法）

merger 合併

account 客戶

time off 休假，休息

Hanukkah 光明節，獻殿節（猶太教的慶典，每年猶太曆9月〈西曆 11~12月〉25日開始，為期八天紀念奪回神殿的節慶）

tied up at work 被工作綁住，忙於工作

與休假有關的說法

 請聽《Track 22》。

1. A: I'm planning to have a vacation in the Caribbean.

   B: That's wonderful. I wish I could go, too.

2. A: What will you be doing during the Christmas vacation?

   B: I'll be vacationing at a ski resort in Switzerland.

3. A: Excuse me. Is Mr. Harris in today?

   B: He is on vacation in France now.

解說

● 「休假」的慣用句是 have/get a vacation，若再加上 planning to （正計劃要）及地名，就是一句漂亮的英文句子。如正計劃要在加勒比海度假，可說成 I'm planning to have a vacation in the Caribbean.。另外，「有給薪假」是 take a vacation with pay 或 take a paid vacation。

● vacation不只當名詞，也能當動詞，表「休假」「度假」之意。當要表達將在瑞士的滑雪勝地度假時，可以說成 I'll be vacationing at a ski resort in Switzerland，而已在歐洲度假過了，則說 We vacationed in Europe.。

● 「在度假」是 on vacation，留意 vacation 之前不加 a 或 the。

練習 1 【代換】

請隨《Track 23》做代換練習。

1. I'm planning to have a vacation in Europe this summer.

Florida this winter.
Mexico this spring.
the Caribbean this fall.
Hawaii this winter.

2. I'll be vacationing in Italy this summer.

at a lake in Virginia this spring.
at a ski resort in Maine this winter.
on a small island in New York this fall.
in Boston this summer.

練習 2 【角色扮演】

請隨《Track 24》在嗶一聲後唸出灰色部分的句子。

1. A: I'm planning to have a vacation in Holland this summer.
   B: That's wonderful. I wish I could go, too.

2. A: What will you be doing during the Christmas vacation?
   B: I'll be vacationing in Hawaii.

3. A: Hello. May I speak to Dr. Leach?
   B: He is on vacation now.

實力測驗

今天有公司的同事問你 What will you be doing during the Christmas vacation?，你內心在想：將和妻子及孩子們在巴哈馬度假三天後，再到紐約探望父母親。請用英語說出這個度假計劃。

| 參考解答 | I'll be vacationing in the Bahamas with my wife and children for three days and then we'll go up to New York to see my parents. |

Chapter 5	**Shopping**	購　物

Listening

Warm-up / Pre-questions

 請聽《Track 25》的會話後回答下面問題。

這位女士正在買什麼東西?

  (A) 女兒的生日禮物

  (B) 要給男朋友的 CD 唱盤

  (C) 要送朋友的禮物

解答   (C)

聽力技巧

1. 掌握重音位置

單音節只有一個母音,所以重音也只有一個;但雙音節以上的字由於有兩個以上的母音,所以會有主重音和次重音之分,必須留意其重音位置的不同。

1 單音節的字:

street [strit] / trend [trɛnd]

2 雙音節以上的字:

manager [`mænɪdʒɚ] / volunteer [ˌvɑlənˈtɪr]

stadium [`stedɪəm] / media [`midɪə]

練習 1

◎ 請聽《Track 26》並在括弧內填入正確答案。

1. Excuse me. Can I speak to the (　　　　)?
2. You can wait in the (　　　　).
3. You'll end up in big (　　　　).

> 解答　　　1. Excuse me. Can I speak to the (manager)?
> 2. You can wait in the (studio).
> 3. You'll end up in big (trouble).

2. 留意字的拼法 ……字尾以子音結束／弱音節的母音微弱發音／連續同一個子音

英文是「字母式」語言，是由字母串成單字，由字母音變化構成單字的音，所以英語的字母與聲音之間是有差距的。在我們背單字時，除了要熟悉正確發音之外，最好也留意單字的正確拼法，將有助於記憶與閱讀。

1 字尾以子音結束：

gram [græm] / tenant [ˋtɛnənt]

2 弱音節的母音微弱發音：

chocolate [ˋtʃɔklɪt] / image [ˋɪmɪdʒ]

3 連續同一個子音：

hammer [ˋhæmɚ] / tunnel [ˋtʌnl]

練習 2

◎ 請聽《Track 27》並在括弧內填入正確答案。

1. We're looking for a (　　　　).
2. Would you like some (　　　　)?
3. Will you pass me the (　　　　), please?

解答	1. We're looking for a (tenant).
	2. Would you like some (chocolate)?
	3. Will you pass me the (hammer), please?

Listening Quiz

請聽《Track 25》的會話後回答下面問題。

女士除了 CD 唱盤外，還買了什麼？

(A) 喇叭和耳機

(B) 喇叭和幾張 CD

(C) 攜帶式手提包和頭戴型耳機

(D) 喇叭和頭戴型耳機

解答 (D)

Speaking

會話

請再聽一次《Track 25》。

A: Can I help you find something?

B: I'm looking for a CD player for my friend, but I don't know what kind to get.

A. Oh, I will be happy to help you with that. Do you want a portable CD player or a stationary one?

B: It would be nice if she could take it with her when she travels, but be able to play it at home with speakers as well.

A: I think she would enjoy this one. It is portable, but you can attach these little speakers to it and play it at home.

B: Oh, that's really convenient. I like that. What kind of headset comes with this?

A: Only these little earphones, but we have a really nice set of headphones on sale. Try these on.

B: Oh, yes, they sound great. I am pleased with your selections. How much does all of this cost?

A: Well, it's your lucky day because everything you want is on sale. The CD player is only $60.00, the speakers are $25.00, and the headphones are $23.00, for a total of $108.00 plus tax.

B: That is not bad. I will take all three of them. Can you gift-wrap them?

A: Certainly. Will that be cash, check, or charge?

中譯

A: 需要我幫您找什麼東西嗎?

B: 我正在為朋友找一台 CD 唱盤，不過不知道該選哪一種好。

A: 我很高興能為您服務。您要攜帶式的還是要固定型的 CD 唱盤?

B: 最好是既可以讓她在旅行時隨身攜帶，又可以在家中用喇叭播放出來的。

A: 我想她應該會喜歡這一款。這一款不但可以隨身攜帶，而且只需插接這種小型喇叭就可以在家中播放了。

B: 嗯，這真的很方便，我喜歡。這一款是搭配哪一種耳機呢?

A: 是這一組迷你型耳機,不過我們現在有另外一組相當不錯的耳機正在特價中,您可以試聽看看。

B: 喔,對,這組音效聽起來很棒。你介紹的組合我都很滿意,這些總共是多少錢?

A: 您今天的運氣很不錯,您要的每一樣東西都剛好有特價。CD唱盤只要 60 美元,喇叭是 25 美元,再加上耳機 23 美元,含稅總共是 108 美元。

B: 並不算貴,這三樣我都要了。你能將它們包裝得漂亮嗎?

A: 沒問題。請問您要付現、開支票,還是刷卡?

關鍵字

stationary　安裝好的,固定住的

headset　頭戴式(含麥克風)耳機(有時亦同 headphone 之意)

on sale　特價,拍賣

gift-wrap　將～包裝成禮物

Will that be cash, check, or charge?　請問您要付現、開支票,還是刷卡?

購物的說法

 請聽《Track 28》。

1. A: May I help you?

   B: Yes. I'm looking for a handbag.

2. A: Can I help you find something?

   B: No, thank you. I am just looking right now.

3. A: Will you show me that doll on the shelf?

B: Sure. Which one?

解說

● May I help you?（我可以為您服務嗎）及 What can I do for you, sir/madam?（先生/女士，有什麼需要為您服務的嗎）相當於我們這裡一進店門，店員馬上開口說的「歡迎光臨」之意；但由於是疑問句，顧客在禮貌上還是須有所回應。若是已有明確的購物目標，可說如 Yes, I'm looking for a handbag.（嗯，我想要找手提包）或 I'd like to see some T-shirts.（我想要看看T恤）的句子。

● 若只是進店裡隨意逛逛，在一聽到店員說 May I help you? 時，可以回答 No, thank you. I'm just looking right now.（不用麻煩，我只是看看）。

● 在店裡想要看架子上或展示櫃裡的物品時，可用 Will you...? 的請求句型詢問，即說 Will you show me that doll on the self?。若想要試穿衣服，則說 May I try this on?；決定買了就說 I'll buy this one. 或 I'll take this one.。

練習 1【代換】

 請隨《Track 29》做代換練習。

　　1. I'm looking for a CD player.
<blockquote>
a handbag.

a leather jacket.

a suitcase.

a pair of earrings.
</blockquote>

2. Will you show me this watch?

> that vase on the shelf?
> that camera in the showcase?
> something else?
> some other blouses?

練習 2 【角色扮演】

請隨《Track 30》在嗶一聲後唸出灰色部分的句子。

1. A: May I help you?

   B: Yes. I'm looking for a pair of sneakers.

2. A: Can I help you find something?

   B: No, thank you. I am just looking right now.

3. A: Will you show me that clock on the shelf?

   B: Sure. Which one?

實力測驗

> 你要買一份禮物送給朋友，但正傷腦筋不知買什麼好，於是就想先進禮品店瞧瞧，一進門，店員就親切地對你說 Can I help you find something?，這時你會如何請求幫忙呢？

參考解答　Yes, please. I'm looking for a gift for my friend, but I don't know what to buy.

Chapter		
6	**Talking About Traffic**	談交通

Listening

Warm-up / Pre-questions

◎ 請聽《Track 31》的會話後回答下面問題。

> Mary 和 Betty 為什麼會上班遲到?
>
> (A) 沒趕上電車
>
> (B) 路上塞車
>
> (C) 睡過頭
>
> ――――――――――――――――――――――――
> 解答　　　　　　　　　　　　　　　　　　　(B)

聽力技巧

1. 聽懂片語⑴……介系詞 + 名詞（+ 介系詞）

所謂片語是由兩個以上的單字組成，其意義多少已經和各個單字的原本意義不同，具有特定的意思。外國人在日常生活中，經常會使用片語，並且通常將其視為一個單字發音，所以我們在聽的時候，難免會受到混淆，不易聽懂。建議練習時，不要將片語的單字分得一清二楚，而是應將其視作一個單字。若按詞性，可將片語分成幾種形式，在此先練習聽懂「介系詞 + 名詞（+ 介系詞）」的片語。

「介系詞 + 名詞（+ 介系詞）」的例子:

in all（全部）/ for a while（一會兒）/ at a time（一次）/ in order to（為了～）/ in front of（在～之前）/ on account of（由於～）

練習 1

請聽《Track 32》並在括弧內填入一個片語。

1. The plane will arrive (　　　　).

2. (　　　　), the quality is very poor.

3. Who is (　　　) this store?

解答

1. The plane will arrive (on time).

2. (On top of it), the quality is very poor.

3. Who is (in charge of) this store?

2. 聽懂片語 (2)……動詞 + 形容詞

外國人在日常會話中，也經常會用到「動詞 + 形容詞」形式的片語。記得唸的時候，不論動詞或形容詞，都必須加強重音。

「動詞 + 形容詞」的例子：

make sure（確認）/ stand still（站著不動）/ feel free（隨意）/ feel bad（感到歉疚）/ leave alone（不管）

練習 2

請聽《Track 33》並在括弧內填入一個片語。

1. The two lanes (　　　　) for 20 minutes.

2. Please (　　　) to ask questions.

3. I'll (　　　) that he gets the message.

解答

1. The two lanes (sat still) for 20 minutes.

2. Please (feel free) to ask questions.

3. I'll (make sure) that he gets the message.

Listening Quiz

 請聽《Track 31》的會話後回答下面問題。

道路除施工外，還因什麼原因塞車?

  (A) 下大雨

  (B) 刮颱風

  (C) 發生車禍

  (D) 有遊行

解答   (C)

═══ Speaking ═══

會話

請再聽一次《Track 31》。

A: Mary, please forgive me. I am so sorry that I am late for work. Traffic was unbelievable!

B: It's all right, Betty. I was late this morning, too. I just got here. Did you take the 805?

A: I sure did. They had two lanes closed for road repair. Can you imagine them doing that during rush hour?

B: I know. It's ridiculous. On top of it, I don't know when you left your house, but at about 6: 30 there was an accident, too! All three other lanes just sat still for 30 minutes while they moved the wreckage to the roadside.

A: I know that is awful. Traffic was still backed up when I got to that point. I heard on the radio that two people were seriously injured.

B: Yes, I heard that, too. How sad!

A: Well, it sounds like we need to find a new route to work.

B: I think so. I am going to leave about 15 minutes earlier tomorrow and take the 5 instead. It should be clear that early in the morning.

A: That sounds like a good idea. I will probably do that as well. Do you know how long they will be working on the freeway?

B: I saw a big orange caution sign that said April 1–April 30.

A: A whole month! What an inconvenience!

中譯

A: 瑪莉，真是對不起，我遲到了，請原諒我。交通狀況實在是糟透了！

B: 貝蒂，沒關係，我也遲到了，才剛到而已。妳是搭805號公車來的嗎？

A: 對呀。由於道路整修的關係，有兩條車道被封閉了。真令人不敢相信他們竟然選在交通尖峰時刻這麼做！

B: 是啊，真是荒謬。我不知道妳是什麼時候出門的，不過六點半左右的時候還發生了交通事故呢！為了清除車禍現場，其他的三條車道也通通靜止了30分鐘。

A: 沒錯，那真是很糟糕。當我到達那裡時，交通也還是很堵塞。我在收音機裡還聽見有兩個人嚴重受傷呢。

B：是啊，我也聽說了，真是不幸！

A：看樣子我們必須找一條新路線上班了。

B：沒錯。明天開始，我會提早 15 分鐘出門改搭 5 號公車。一大早的路況應該會不錯吧。

A：這是個好主意，我大概也會這麼做。妳知道高速公路要施工多久嗎？

B：我看到一個大大的橘色標示牌上寫著 4 月 1 日到 4 月 30 日。

A：竟然要整整一個月！真是太不方便了！

關鍵字

Traffic was unbelievable!　交通狀況糟糕到令人難以置信的地步。

the 805　805 號公車

ridiculous　荒謬

on top of it　再加上

sit still　靜止不動

wreckage　殘骸，碎片

roadside　路邊

be backed up　（交通）阻塞

it sounds like　聽起來像，似乎是

as well　同樣，也（和 too 同義）

freeway　高速公路

與交通有關的說法

◎ 請聽《Track 34》。

1. A: Do you go to work by car?

   B: No, I go to work by subway.

2. A: I'm sorry I was late. I was caught in a traffic jam.

   B: That's all right. You weren't too late.

3. A: Traffic is backed up for miles.

   B: Can we take another route?

解說

● 表利用某種交通工具的說法中，如 by car 及 by train 等，在 by 之後不須加 a 或 the 的冠詞；但若是要搭某特定時間的交通工具時，則須加定冠詞，例如 go by the 3 o'clock train（搭 3 點的列車）。搭乘某交通工具上班的英文除了「by + 交通工具」的說法外，也可以說成如 I take the train daily to work.或 I commute from Paterson to Manhattan every day.（我每天從帕特遜通勤到曼哈頓）的句子。

● 「交通阻塞」是 traffic congestion，或是 traffic jam；「我遇上交通阻塞」的英文即是 I was caught in a traffic jam. 或 I was stuck in a traffic jam for one hour.。另外，「道路塞車」是 The street is congested with cars.；「塞了好幾公里」是 Traffic is backed up for miles.；「交通壅塞得很嚴重」則是 Traffic is bumper-to-bumper.。

練習 1 【代換】

 請隨《Track 35》做代換練習。

1. I go to work by car.

> train.
> subway.
> bus.
> bicycle.

2. Traffic is backed up for miles.

> is very heavy now.
> is very congested.
> gets bad just before 7 o'clock.
> seems to be clearing.

練習 2 【角色扮演】

 請隨《Track 36》在嗶一聲後唸出灰色部分的句子。

1. A: Do you drive to work?

 B: No, I go to work by bus.

2. A: How come you were late this morning?

 B: I was caught in traffic jam.

3. A: Traffic is backed up for miles.

 B: Let's get off the speed way at the next exit.

實力測驗

今天早上你因路上發生車禍而上班遲到了，老闆非常不高興，怒氣沖沖地問你是怎麼回事，這時你要如何解釋呢？

參考解答　　There was an accident and I was caught in a
traffic jam.

Chapter 7 | Hotel Check-in 旅館登記住宿

Listening

Warm-up / Pre-questions

請聽《Track 37》的會話後回答下面問題。

Schultz 要在旅館待幾天？

(A) 3 天

(B) 4 天

(C) 5 天

解答   (C)

聽力技巧

1. 聽懂片語 (3)……**動詞 + 副詞 / 介系詞**

動詞和副詞，或動詞和介系詞結合成片語後，通常會有新的意思產生。另外，由於動詞的最後一個子音會和副詞或介系詞的第一個音連在一起唸，所以聽起來往往會像是一個單字。

「動詞 + 副詞 / 介系詞」的例子：

fill out（填寫）/ set up（設立）/ stand by（待命）/ think of（考慮）/ get across（使理解）/ look through（粗略過目）

練習 1

請聽《Track 38》並在括弧內填入一個片語。

　　1. Will you please (　　　　　　) the application form?

2. I have to (　　　　　) the proposal next Wednesday.

3. Will you (　　　　　) the report?

解答　1. Will you please (fill out) the application form?

2. I have to (hand in) the proposal next Wednesday.

3. Will you (look through) the report?

2. 聽懂片語 (4)……動詞＋名詞＋介系詞、形容詞＋副詞／介系詞

「動詞＋名詞＋介系詞」也是經常出現的一種片語形式，秘訣同樣是將三個字連在一起視為一個單字發音。「形容詞＋副詞／介系詞」片語則要留意形容詞字尾的子音與副詞、介系詞字首的音的連結。

「動詞＋名詞＋介系詞」的例子：

take care of（照顧）／ take advantage of（利用）／

make use of（使用）／ make fun of（嘲笑）

「形容詞＋副詞／介系詞」的例子：

tired of（厭煩）／ used to（習慣）／ pleased with（滿意）

練習 2

請聽《Track 39》並在括弧內填入一個片語。

1. I'll (　　　　　) it.

2. I'm not (　　　　　) this type of photocopier.

3. I'm (　　　　　) answering the phone.

解答　1. I'll (take care of) it.

2. I'm not (familiar with) this type of photocopier.

3. I'm (tired of) answering the phone.

Listening Quiz

請聽《Track 37》的會話後回答下面問題。

Schultz 在櫃檯詢問什麼事?

    (A) 行李員是否可幫忙將行李搬進房間

    (B) 房間內是否可以上網

    (C) 商務中心幾點開始服務

    (D) 沒有事先預訂好房間是否可以住進旅館

解答   (B)

=== **Speaking** ===

會話

請再聽一次《Track 37》。

A: Hello and welcome to the Westin Royal Hotel. May I help you?

B: My name is James Schultz. I have a reservation for a room for five nights.

A: Just a moment, please. Yes, Mr. Schultz, a single room for five nights, leaving on Monday, November 18th.

B: That's right.

A: Will you fill out the register, please?

B: Sure. (*A moment later*) Here you are.

A: Thank you. Your room is 2315. Here's your key. Do you have any luggage?

B: Yes, just one suitcase.

A: Would you like the bellboy to bring it to your room?

B: Yes, that'd be nice. Oh, can I access the Internet in the room?

A: Yes, just plug your phone line directly into a wall telephone jack and program your computer to dial 9 for an outside line.

B: Great. Is there a business center in your hotel?

A: Yes, it's on this floor just around the corner between the gift shop and the restaurant.

中譯

A: 您好！歡迎光臨威斯登皇家飯店。我能為您服務嗎？

B: 我的名字是詹姆士‧舒茲。我有預訂一個房間待五個晚上。

A: 請稍等一下。是的，舒茲先生，您有預訂一間單人房住五個晚上，預計11月18日星期一離開。

B: 沒錯。

A: 請您先填好住宿登記簿。

B: 好的。（過了一會）填好了。

A: 謝謝。您的房間是 2315 號房，這是您的鑰匙。您有攜帶行李嗎？

B: 有，只有一個皮箱。

A: 您需要行李員將行李送到房間嗎？

B: 嗯，好啊。喔，請問房間內可以撥接上網嗎？

A: 可以，您只需將電話線直接接入牆上的電話匣，並連接電腦再撥 9 打外線即可。

B: 太好了。飯店內有商務中心嗎？

A: 有，就在這層樓的禮品店與餐廳之間的轉角。

關鍵字

register　住宿登記簿

luggage　行李

bellboy　行李員（旅館內主要負責搬運行李的男服務生）

outside line　外線

business center　商務中心（電腦、影印機等辦公設備齊全，提供傳真、影印等服務的地方）

旅館住宿的說法

 請聽《Track 40》。

1. A: Hotel Claremont. May I help you?

   B: I'd like to reserve a single room for three nights from May 17th.

2. A: May I help you?

   B: My name is Tom Glazer. I have a reservation for a room tonight.

3. A: Front Desk. May I help you?

   B: This is Clara Jones in Room 2356. I'd like to extend my stay until the day after tomorrow. I'll be leaving on Wednesday.

解說

● 向旅館預約房間，一開頭可說 I'd like to reserve a room，其後再補充住宿的天數及日期。例如要從 5 月 17 日起住三晚，可說 I'd like to reserve a room for three nights from May 17th.。而

當對方詢問 What kind of room would you like? 時，可回答 A single room. 或 A twin room.。

● 到達旅館後，必須在櫃檯辦理住宿登記手續。首先報上姓名，例如說 My name is Tom Glazer.，再說明預約的內容：I have a reservation for a room tonight.。 若是要住宿多天則說 I have a reservation for a room from tonight to Wednesday.。

● 要延長住宿可用 extend my stay until 的說法，並且最好明確說出離開的時間或日期，例如 I'll be leaving on Wednesday.，這樣可以避免引起誤解。

練習 1 【代換】

請隨《Track 41》做代換練習。

1. **I would like to** reserve a single room for one night on July 6th.

> reserve a single room for two nights on August 5th and 6th.
> reserve a single room for three nights from September 12th.
> extend my stay until Thursday this week.
> extend my stay for two more nights. I'll be leaving on Friday.

2. I have a reservation for a room for tonight.

> a single room for tonight.
> a twin room for tonight and tomor-row.
> a room for three nights.
> a suite for a week.

練習 2 【角色扮演】

 請隨《Track 42》在嗶一聲後唸出灰色部分的句子。

1. A: Hotel Claremont. May I help you?

    B: I'd like to reserve a single room for two nights on November 16th and 17th.

2. A: May I help you?

    B: My name is Florence Morrow. I have a reservation for a room for two nights.

3. A: Front Desk. May I help you?

    B: This is Steve Hamilton in Room 2748. I'd like to extend my stay for three more nights. I'll be leaving on Thursday.

實力測驗

你事先沒有跟旅館預訂房間，但仍想問能不能住個兩晚，你要如何跟櫃檯人員說呢？

參考解答　Hi. I don't have a reservation, but I wonder if I can have a room for two nights.

Seeing the Doctor　　看醫生

Listening

Warm-up / Pre-questions

　請聽《Track 43》的會話後回答下面問題。

Michael 生了什麼病?

(A) 胃炎

(B) 盲腸炎

(C) 輕微感冒

解答　　　　　　　　　　　　　　　　　　　　　　　　　(C)

聽力技巧

1. 抓住重音 (1)……**不易分辨重音位置的單字和詞語**

英語的重音位置非常重要,外國人經常就是以重音位置來抓住
單字的意思。中文是每個字有每個字本身的發音,若聽不清楚
對方某些字的音,往往就會雞同鴨講、不知所云;但英語則不
同,只要重音節唸得正確,即使其他部分發音不清楚,也不會
令人誤解意思。例如某個字的一個音節裡有 a 或 e 的字母,若
該音節未標重音,聽起來就像是 [ə] 音,excellent 即是一例,其
音標為 [ˈɛksḷənt],由於重音在第一音節 e 上,所以只有該處會
清楚發音,其他的 e 則會輕讀。建議背單字時,不要光記中文
意思,應該再熟記重音位置,這一點將有助於奠定聽力的基礎。
另外,數字 one 本身有重音,但當被形容詞修飾變成代名詞的

性質 one（表人或物）時，則不加重音。例如：I'll take this one.
（我要買這個）的句子中，重音落在 this 上，one 會輕微發音。
「形容詞 + 名詞」的詞語則是兩個字都唸重音，但主重音會落
在名詞上。

不易分辨重音位置的單字：

alcohol [ˈælkəˌhɔl] / image [ˈɪmɪdʒ] / interval [ˈɪntɚvl] / olive [ˈɑlɪv] /
percent [pɚˈsɛnt]

「形容詞 + one」的例子：

big one（大的東西）/ small one（小的東西）/ red one（紅色的東
西）

「形容詞 + 名詞」的例子：

good answer（好的答案）/ great time（美好的時光）/ wonderful
job（良好的職業）

練習 1

請聽《Track 44》並在括弧內填入正確答案。

1. How did you (　　　　) to do that?

2. This is nice, but too big. I'll buy the (　　　　).

3. I seem to have a (　　　　).

解答　　1. How did you (manage) to do that?
　　　　2. This is nice, but too big. I'll buy the (smaller one).
　　　　3. I seem to have a (head cold).

2. 抓住重音 (2)……依重音位置不同而造成詞性或意思改變的單字及詞語

即使是相同的英文單字，若重音位置轉移，也會影響到詞性的
改變。另外，像「形容詞 + 名詞」的詞語也會因重音位置的不
同而改變意思。

重音位置不同改變詞性的例子：

export [ˈɛksport] n.（出口） vs. export [ɪksˋport] vt.vi.（輸出）

conduct [ˈkɑndʌkt] n.（行為） vs. conduct [kənˋdʌkt] vt.vi.（引導）

重音位置不同改變意思的例子：

'green‚house （溫室） vs. 'green 'house （綠色的房子）

'high‚chair （高腳的嬰兒進食用椅） vs. 'high 'chair （高的椅子）

練習 2

◎ 請聽《Track 45》並在括弧內填入正確答案。

1. We are looking for a (　　　　　).

2. When shall we (　　　　　) the survey?

3. We grow these plants in a (　　　　　).

解答

1. We are looking for a (suspect).

2. When shall we (conduct) the survey?

3. We grow these plants in a (greenhouse).

Listening Quiz

◎ 請聽《Track 43》的會話後回答下面問題。

針對 Michael 勞累過度的情形，醫生給與什麼建議？

(A) 換工作

(B) 旅行以調適心情

(C) 多吃維他命

(D) 跟公司請幾天假好好休息

解答　　　　　　　　　　　　　　　　　　　　　　　(D)

Speakinging

會話

 請再聽一次《Track 43》。

A: Good afternoon Michael. What brings you to see us today?

B: Well, Dr. Hamilton, for the past few days I haven't been feeling well.

A: What specifically is bothering you?

B: I have a constant cough, a runny nose, my throat is sore, and I feel exhausted.

A: Have you been running a temperature?

B: Just a mild one, around 100 degrees.

A: I see. Let me take a look at your throat. Say "Ah."

B: Ah.

A: Yes, your throat is as red as fire. You have the head cold that has been going around. I'll prescribe a strong cough suppressant and something to dry up your nose for you to take along with your aspirin. About your fatigue, have you been getting enough sleep?

B: No, not really. I have been working overtime for three weeks. I only manage about five hours of sleep a night.

A: My goodness! You need a good rest. I recommend you take a couple of days off and relax.

B: I suppose I really do need a couple of days off of work.

A: If you follow my advice, you will be feeling better in no time.

A: 午安，麥克，今天是為了什麼原因來這裡呀?

B: 唉，漢彌頓醫生，過去這幾天我一直覺得不舒服。

A: 有什麼地方特別不舒服嗎?

B: 我一直不斷咳嗽、流鼻水、喉嚨痛，而且感到疲憊不堪。

A: 有發燒嗎?

B: 有一點，體溫是華氏一百度左右。

A: 我明白了。讓我瞧一瞧你的喉嚨，說「啊」。

B: 啊。

A: 沒錯，你的喉嚨正紅得跟火燄一樣。你得了流行性感冒了。我
   會開給你強效的止咳劑、治鼻水的藥，搭配阿斯匹靈一起服用。
   至於你的疲勞問題，你最近睡眠充足嗎?

B: 不，並沒有。我已經連續加班三個星期了。我一個晚上只能勉
   強湊到五個鐘頭左右的時間睡覺。

A: 我的天啊! 你需要好好地休息一下。我建議你最好請幾天假，
   讓自己放鬆一下。

B: 我想我是真的需要請幾天假，暫時離開工作一陣子。

A: 如果你聽從我的建議，一定能在短時間內恢復的。

關鍵字

What brings you to see us today?　是什麼風把你給吹來了?(詢問對方
   的來意)

feel exhausted　感到非常疲憊

run a temperature　發燒

100 degrees　（此處指）華氏 100 度（相當於攝氏 37~38 度）

going around　在四周；（感冒）流行

prescribe　開處方

suppressant　抑制劑

take along with　搭配著～一起服用

aspirin　阿斯匹靈

work overtime　工作超時

a couple of days off　休息數日（約 2~3 天）

看病的說法

 請聽《Track 46》。

1. A: Alexandria Hospital. May I help you?

   B: I'd like to make an appointment to see a doctor today.

2. A: What's the problem?

   B: I have a high fever.

3. A: What symptoms do you have?

   B: I have been coughing all day.

解說

● 預約掛號看診的說法是 I'd like to make an appointment to see a doctor.；若想要在特定的日期看診，可在句子之後加上希望看病的日期，說成如 I'd like to make an appointment to see a doctor this Wednesday. 的句子。掛急診則說 Could I see a doctor right now? This is an emergency.。

● What's the problem? 及 What seems to be the problem? 是醫生、護士詢問病人「哪邊不舒服」的慣用句。英語通常使用 have

一字來說明病症，如罹患感冒就說 I have a cold.；頭痛說 I have a headache.；發高燒則說 I have a high fever. 等。想表達症狀「嚴重」，可使用 bad 修飾，例如說成 I have a bad headache.。另外，一些常見的病症說法如下：

a cold（感冒）/ a headache（頭痛）/ a stomachache（肚子痛）/ a toothache（牙痛）/ a backache（腰痛）/ sore eyes（眼睛痛）/ sore throat（喉嚨痛）

● What symptoms do you have? 是醫生詢問病患「有哪些症狀」的慣用句。要敘述身體感到痛時，可先說 I have a pain，再接著描述痛的部位，例如 in the back（背部）。另外「咳嗽」「嘔吐」「輕微發燒」「倦怠」的英文分別是 coughing, throwing up, feverish, sluggish；「我拉肚子」則說 I've been suffering from diarrhea.。

練習 1【代換】

 請隨《Track 47》做代換練習。

　1. **I have** a bad headache.

> a bad stomachache.
> a keen pain in my back.
> a high fever and have been coughing all day.
> a high fever and have been throwing up since last night.

2. I have been coughing all day.

> throwing up since last night.
> feverish for the past three days.
> feeling sluggish all day.
> suffering from diarrhea since last night.

練習 2【角色扮演】

 請隨《Track 48》在嗶一聲後唸出灰色部分的句子。

1. A: Alexandria Hospital. May I help you?

   B: I'd like to make an appointment to see a doctor this morning.

2. A: What's the problem?

   B: I have a bad headache.

3. A: What symptoms do you have?

   B: I have been feverish for the past few days.

實力測驗

你感冒了！發高燒又嚴重咳嗽，鼻水也流個不停。你要怎麼跟外國醫生說明這些症狀呢？

參考解答　　I have a high fever and have been coughing all day. My nose is constantly running.

Business Lunch　商業午餐

Listening

Warm-up / Pre-questions

請聽《Track 49》的會話後回答下面問題。

Richard 和 George 在哪裡?

(A) 公司附近的餐廳

(B) 建築工地

(C) 速食店

解答 (A)

聽力技巧

1. 抓住語調 (1)……強調單字的意思

所謂語調，是指說英語時，句子音調的高低起伏，以及語氣的抑揚頓挫。例如：Do you smoke? 其句尾音調上揚，是疑問句；I smoke. 的句尾音調下降，則是直述句。另外，語調更有強調重要單字意思的功能。請看下面的例子：

I went to the museum with Nancy yesterday.

這句話的重音通常在 went, museum, Nancy, yesterday 等字，語調最高的音則落在 went 上，之後慢慢下降，到 yesterday 時是最低。

I went to the museum with Nancy yesterday.

● ● ● ● ● ● ● ●

不過，若要強調「是我去，不是其他人」時，則在 I 最高，即加

強 I 的音，其後平穩下降。

I went to the museum with Nancy yesterday.

● ● · · ● ● · ● · ● ·

又，若要加強 museum[mjuˈziəm] 時，則在該字加強 [i] 的重音，
其後平穩下降。

我們若能正確抓住語調，就能正確理解說話者話的意思及其微
妙的心情。

練習 1

◎ 請聽《Track 50》並在括弧內填入正確答案。

1. I'm having a cup of coffee. What are (　　　) having?

2. I didn't order beef. I ordered (　　　).

3. I had lunch with Nancy (　　　).

解答	1. I'm having a cup of coffee. What are (you) having?
	2. I didn't order beef. I ordered (chicken).
	3. I had lunch with Nancy (yesterday).

2. 抓住語調 (2)……不同意思的 Yes

同是回答對方問句作肯定答覆的 Yes，若改變語調，就會有以下
不同的語意產生。

1. 最常見到的是語調下降的 Yes [↘]，是肯定回答「是，沒錯」
的意思。

"Do you play tennis?" "Yes."

2. 語調上揚的 Yes [↗]，是用來回應他人的呼喚，或鼓勵催促
對方繼續談話。

"Tom!" "Yes?"

"I talked to Helen this morning." "Yes?"

3. 語調先下降再上揚的 Yes [↘↗]，有暗示其他的意思，表示「是
的，不過…」之意。

"Do you like this car?" "Yes." (Yes, but it's too expensive for me.)

4. 語調先上揚再下降的Yes [↷]，表示驚訝、感動，有「當然」的強調之意。

"Did you enjoy the game?" "Yes."

練習2

請聽《Track 51》並從下面選項選出 **Yes** 的正確用法。

1. "Do you ski?" "Yes." (　　)

2. "John called me from New York this morning." "Yes?" (　　)

3. "Did you like the food?" "Yes." (　　)

[Yes 的正確意思]

(A) 是的，不過…

(B) 是的，沒錯（Yes 的一般用法）

(C) 當然（Yes 的強調用法）

(D) 然後呢（鼓勵對方繼續說下去）

解答	
	1. (B)
	2. (D)
	3. (A)

Listening Quiz

 請聽《Track 49》的會話後回答下面問題。

Richard 和 George 開始談論什麼話題?

(A) 印度的文化

(B) 印度的經濟

(C) 印度的電腦市場

(D) 印度的咖哩

解答 (C)

Speaking

會話

 請再聽一次《Track 49》。

A: This is a nice little restaurant, Richard. The menu looks very appetizing.

B: I love this place. I make it a point to come here when I am buried with work. The food is great and it is close enough to work that I don't feel guilty leaving my desk.

A: Have you ever had the Marsala-Marinara Linguini?

B: It is one of my favorites. It has tender chicken pieces with linguini and mushrooms covered in a tomato and Marsala wine sauce with cheese on top.

A: That sounds great. I think I will have that. What are you having?

B: I think I am going to have the Tai Linguini. I really like their spicy Thai peanut-ginger sauce.

C: Are you gentlemen ready to order?

A: Yes, I will have the Marsala-Marinara Linguini and iced tea, please.

B: And I will have the Thai Linguini with a diet coke.

C: Thank you. I will get your orders right to you.

B: So what were the results of your market research in India, George?

A: The results are positive. It looks like the computer market will grow about 10 times its current size within the next two years.

中譯

A： 理查，這家小餐廳很不錯，這菜單看起來就讓人胃口大開。

B： 我很喜歡這家餐廳。每當我被工作壓得透不過氣時，就會到這裡來。這裡的食物美味可口，地點又不會離辦公室太遠，因此不會讓我有逃離工作的罪惡感。

A： 你有吃過這裡的馬沙拉蒜香蕃茄麵嗎？

B： 那是我最喜愛的義大利麵之一呢。那是在鮮嫩的雞肉，以及義大利寬扁細麵與蘑菇之上，澆淋蕃茄混合馬沙拉酒的醬汁後再加上一層起司而成。

A： 聽起來很美味。我想我就點這道了，你呢？

B： 我要點泰式義大利麵。我非常喜歡他們的花生與薑味的泰式辣醬。

C: 請問兩位男士可以點餐了嗎?

A: 可以,我要點馬沙拉蒜香蕃茄麵和冰紅茶。

B: 我要泰式義大利麵和健怡可樂。

C: 好的,謝謝。餐點將會儘快送上。

B: 對了,喬治,你的印度市場的調查結果怎麼樣?

A: 調查結果非常樂觀,印度的電腦市場預計將在兩年內成長十倍。

關鍵字

appetizing　開胃的,促進食慾的

make it a point to　經常,必定

buried with work　被工作壓得透不過氣來

Marsala　馬沙拉白葡萄酒(義大利西西里島生產的開胃甜烈酒)

Marinara　大蒜蕃茄醬(一種義大利調味醬,用蕃茄、大蒜和香辛料調製而成)

Linguini　義大利寬扁細麵

favorite　特別喜愛的東西

Thai　泰國的

diet coke　健怡可樂(無糖低卡的飲料)

positive　建設性的,有希望的

餐廳用餐的說法

 請聽《Track 52》。

1. A: How many people do you have in your party?

   B: There are two of us.

2. A: May I take your order?

   B: I'll have a Caesar Salad and Sirloin Steak.

3. A: Excuse me. Could I have more water, please?

   B: Sure. I'll be right with you.

解說

● 大部分英美餐廳的服務生會在門口詢問：How many people do you have in your party? （請問有幾位），若是只有自己一個人用餐即說 Just myself.；兩個人用餐則說 There are two of us.。

● 坐在餐位後不久，會有男服務生或女服務生上前詢問：May I take your order? （可以點餐了嗎），有時也會聽到 Are you ready to order? 的問句。點菜的開頭慣用句型是 I'll have...，例如：I'll have a Caesar Salad and Sirloin Steak. （我要點凱撒沙拉和沙朗牛排）。若未決定好要點的菜，可先說 I'm not ready to order yet. Could you give me a few more minutes, please?，請服務生等候。

● 想請服務生多加水或咖啡的慣用句是 Could I have more water / coffee, please?。用完餐後，想請服務生將帳單送到自己的餐桌上時，可說 Could/Can I have my check, please?。

練習 1 【代換】

◎ 請隨《Track 53》做代換練習。

1. I'll have a Steak Sandwich and a glass of Coke.

   Seafood Pizza and a cup of coffee.
   a Caesar Salad and Sirloin Steak.
   Eggdrop Soup and Sweet and Sour Pork.
   the Soup of the Day and Coconut Shrimp.

2. Excuse me. Could I have more water, please?

more coffee, please?
another glass of wine, please?
another glass of beer, please?
my check, please?

練習 2【角色扮演】

 請隨《Track 54》在嗶一聲後唸出灰色部分的句子。

1. A: How many people do you have in your party?

B: Just myself.

2. A: May I take your order?

B: I'll have a Caesar Salad and Lobster Tail.

3. A: Excuse me. Could I have another glass of wine, please?

B: Sure. That was a chardonnay, correct?

實力測驗

你正在一家雅致的餐廳內，看著菜單想點些美味可口的食物來享用。不久有位服務生過來詢問你要點哪些菜，請你就下列點選三樣食物回答。

French Onion Soup, Potato Soup, Caesar Salad, Bay Shrimp Salad, Fish and Chips, Spaghetti and Meatballs, Grilled Salmon, Red Wine, White Wine, Beer, Coke

參考解答　I'll have a Caesar Salad, Spaghetti, and a glass of red wine.

Listening

Warm-up / Pre-questions

請聽《Track 55》的會話後回答下面問題。

影印機是哪裡故障?

(A) 無法雙面影印

(B) 卡紙

(C) 無法順利放大或縮小影印

解答 (B)

聽力技巧

1. 掌握節奏 (1)……留意重音位置的所在

英文不只單字有重音,連句子的音調也有明顯強弱的不同。例如句子中意思比較重要的字詞常會加強發音,而其他字詞則會輕微帶過。若要掌握所聽到的內容,就必須留意加強重音的地方。其實,英語的強讀及弱讀的地方皆有特定的形式,並由此創造出英語富有節奏的特色。若能了解英語節奏的基本型態,相信必能提升聽力。

1. Try hard.
　● ●

2. I got it.
　● ● ●

3. Pick it up.
  ● ● ●

4. He came with us.
  ● ● ● ●

5. What did you do?
  ● ● ● ●

6. I gave it to him.
  ● ● ● ●

7. She locked the door.
  ● ● ● ●

8. It started to rain.
  ● ● ● ●

9. Put it on the floor.
  ● ● ● ●

10. I like it better.
  ● ● ● ●

練習 1

◎ 請聽《Track 56》並在括弧內填入正確答案。

1. (　　　) at (　　　).

2. I (　　　) to her.

3. (　　　) it on the (　　　).

解答	
	1. (Look) at (that).
	2. I (spoke) to her.
	3. (Put) it on the (desk).

2. 掌握節奏 (2)……留意沒有唸重音的地方

英文句子中會加強重音的字詞通常是名詞、動詞、形容詞、副詞及疑問詞等內容字(content word)；而會輕微發音的字詞是人稱代名詞(I, you...)、be動詞、介系詞、連接詞及關係詞(who, which...)等功能字(function word)。由於上述的功能字不僅輕微發音，還會唸得很快，所以在聽的時候必須留意。若是能掌握

「答答答答答答」的快速節奏，相信更能幫助我們聽懂英語。

1. I've heard of it before.
    ●   ●   ● ●   ●

2. I wanted to talk to him.
   ● ●   ● ●   ● ●

3. He doesn't want to talk about it.
   ●   ●   ● ● ●   ● ● ●

4. Tell him not to be late.
      ●   ●   ● ● ● ●

5. I think he wants to rest.
   ● ●   ●   ●   ● ●

6. She isn't the same as before.
    ● ● ● ●   ● ● ●

7. She wanted me to listen to her song.
    ● ● ● ● ● ● ● ● ●

8. I want a glass of water.
   ● ● ● ● ● ● ●

9. I wonder if Nancy has heard of it.
   ● ●   ● ● ● ● ● ●

10. What have you done with the book?
      ● ● ●   ●   ● ● ●

練習 2

◎)) 請聽《Track 57》並在括弧內填入正確答案。

1. (   ) want (   ) glass (   ) wine.

2. (   ) doesn't (   ) (   ) talk (   ) (   ).

3. What (   ) (   ) done (   ) (   ) watch?

<table>
<tr><td>解答</td><td>1. (I) want (a) glass (of) wine.</td></tr>
<tr><td></td><td>2. (She) doesn't (want) (to) talk (about) (it).</td></tr>
<tr><td></td><td>3. What (have) (you) done (with) (the) watch?</td></tr>
</table>

Listening Quiz

請聽《Track 55》的會話後回答下面問題。

修理影印機的人什麼時候會到 Amanda 的公司?

(A) 今天上午

(B) 今天下午

(C) 今天下午 4 點以後

(D) 會話中沒有提到

解答	(D)

Speaking

會話

請再聽一次《Track 55》。

A: Repair Department. This is Jason speaking. How may I help you?

B: Hi, Jason. This is Amanda from Kaplan Company. We are having trouble with our copy machine again.

A: What seems to be the problem?

B: Every time we need to make two-sided copies, we get a paper jam in area C-7.

A: Have you tried to clear the jam?

B: Yes. I have cleared the jam several times and it continues to happen.

A: It sounds like there is a problem with the rollers in the C-7 area. We will need to send a maintenance technician out to fix that.

B: How soon can he get here?

A: We are really busy today. I can't promise someone can be there before 4 p.m.

B: Oh, no. Jason, how are we supposed to function without our copy machine all day?

A: I know that puts you in a difficult situation. You are one of our best customers. Hold the line for a second and let me ask my supervisor what we can do to help you.

B: Thanks, Jason. I really appreciate your extra effort.

中譯

A: 維修部門，我是傑森，有什麼能為您效勞的嗎？

B: 傑森，你好，我是卡布蘭公司的亞曼達。我們公司的影印機又出狀況了。

A: 影印機有什麼問題？

B: 我們只要一使用雙面影印，C-7 的部位就會卡紙。

A: 你們有清除卡紙嗎？

B: 有，我已經清了好幾次，可是同樣的問題一再發生。

A: 聽起來似乎是 C-7 部位的滾軸有問題，必須派一位維修技師到你們公司處理。

B: 他大概多久後會到？

A: 由於我們今天實在很忙，所以不敢保證 4 點以前會有人過去。

B: 不會吧，傑森。一整天沒有影印機要叫我們怎麼正常運作？

A: 我知道這會造成你們很大的困擾。畢竟你們是本公司重要的客戶之一，請稍等一下，讓我問一下我的主管有沒有更好的辦法。

B: 謝了，傑森，很感謝你的大力幫忙。

關鍵字

Repair Department　維修部門
two-side copy　雙面影印
get a paper jam　卡紙，夾紙
area C-7　影印機內部標示 C-7 的部位
function　工作，運作

機器故障的相關說法

 請聽《Track 58》。

1. A: What's bothering you, Jim?

   B: This scanner doesn't work.

2. A: Repair Department. This is Walter Gladstone speaking. How may I help you?

   B: Hi, Walter. This is Ruth Benson from Nicolson Company. We are having trouble with our printer again.

3. A: This overhead projector is not working. Will you fix it, George?

   B: All right. Just a moment.

解說

● 機器故障無法運作的情形，可說 doesn't / don't work，如掃描器故障就說成 The scanner doesn't work.；汽車煞車不靈則說

The brake doesn't work.。另外也可以用 out of order（發生故障）的片語表示，如電話壞了，即說 The telephone is out of order.。當我們想標示機器故障時，也可貼上寫有 "Out of order" 的紙條。

● 機器運作顯得異常，可用 having trouble 表示，如說 We are having trouble with our printer.; 或使用 work 的用法，說成 Our printer doesn't work well.。

● 「修理」動詞的英文有 fix, mend, repair 等字。美國人的日常生活會話中常用 fix，如請人修理錶可直接說 Will you fix the watch?; 要將照相機拿去修理，則說 I'm taking this camera to be fixed. 或 I'm sending this camera for repair.; 要請某人修理則說 I'll have George fix this printer. 之類的句子。

練習 1【代換】

◎ 請隨《Track 59》做代換練習。

1. This scanner   doesn't work.

   This photocopier
   This digital camera
   This telephone
   This vending machine

2. Will you fix this modem?

                      this computer?
                      this clock?
                      this cellular phone?
                      this remote control?

練習 2 【角色扮演】

 請隨《Track 60》在嗶一聲後唸出灰色部分的句子。

1. A: What's bothering you, Jim?

   B: This digital camera doesn't work.

2. A: Repair Department. This is Albert Brian speaking. How may I help you?

   B: Hi. Albert. This is Gloria Newcomb from Garrett Technologies. We are having trouble with our airconditioning system again.

3. A: This photocopier is not working. Will you fix it, George?

   B: All right. Just a moment.

實力測驗

辦公室的掃描器壞了，你想要請人趕快修理好，這時你要怎麼對秘書 Wendy 說呢？

參考解答　Wendy, this scanner isn't working. Will you have it fixed as soon as possible?

自然學習英語動詞——基礎篇

大西泰斗、Paul C. McVay 著／何月華 譯

英語一個動詞動輒八、九個語義，若是硬生生地背誦每一個語義實在不是個好方法。本書以圖畫式的「意象學習法」，幫助你不需過度依賴文字解釋，就能清楚區分每個字彙特有的語感，切實掌握各個字彙不同的涵義，使你脫離機械式死背中文翻譯的夢魘，輕鬆暢遊英語動詞的世界。

自然學習英語動詞——進階篇

大西泰斗、Paul C. McVay 著／林韓菁 譯

本書延續《自然學習英語動詞——基礎篇》的精神，從各個進階動詞的語感出發，藉由親身體會各個動詞所具有的原型意象，幫助你靈活運用英語動詞的各種用法，掌握以英語為母語者的語感。當你把英語語感調整成和外國人士一樣時，脫口說英語將是再自然也不過的事了。

英語喜怒哀樂開口說

大內 博
大內 ジャネット 著 ／ 何信彰 譯

附CD

你是不是「高興的時候」只會用happy、「悲傷的時候」只會用sad，再加上一緊張就什麼話都說不出來呢？我們要如何用英語確切地表達出自己的情感呢？本書依各種不同的場合並搭配如臨實境的對話範例，教你記住適當的英語說法及其之間微妙的差異，讓你能確實感受對方心境，也能豐富自我情感表現的色彩！

黛安的日記1

Ronald Brown 著 ／ 呂亨英 譯

大家都知道，學好英文並不是一件容易輕鬆的事，對年僅九歲、從未接觸過英文的黛安更是如此。本書以流暢道地的英文創作，輔以中肯自然的中譯，記錄一位台灣小女孩的英語學習探險。想不想知道一位完全不懂英文的小女孩如何在美國生存？請來看看這本書吧！

輕鬆高爾夫英語

Marsha Krakower 著／劉明綱 譯

你因為英語會話能力不佳，到海外出差或旅行時，不敢與老外在高爾夫球場上一較高下嗎？本書忠實呈現了高爾夫球場上各種英語對話的原貌，讓你在第一次與老外打球時，便能應對自如！而即使不打高爾夫球的人，也可以從此書得到莫大的收穫，能對高爾夫文化有更深一層的了解。

同步口譯教你聽英語

斎藤なが子 著／劉明綱 譯

到底有沒有什麼方法可以增強英語聽力呢？——答案當然有。

本書為日本一位名同步口譯者的力作，書中提到許多正確聆聽及理解英語的聽力技巧，不僅對日本讀者受用，對於有心精進英語聽力的國內讀者而言，也一樣受益無窮。文中穿插許多作者多年來從事口譯心得的小單元，有志走上口譯之路的人務必一睹為快。

從身旁事物開始學習的
生活英語

古藤晃 著／本局編輯部 譯

每天食、衣、住、行所接觸到的事物，你知道如何用英語表達嗎？藉由學習身旁各種事物的英文說法，並在實際生活中不斷地應用，能使英文的生活用語自然而然地留在腦海裡，這絕對是最具效果的英文學習法。想要有效加強生活英語會話能力的你，千萬不可錯過。

動態英語文法

阿部一 著／張慧敏 譯

翻開市面上的英語文法書，可以發現大部分都是文法規則說明，繁而雜的文法概念、生硬的解說，真是令人望而生怯，難道文法只能用這種方式學習嗎？請你不妨打開本書看看，作者是以談天的方式，生動地為你解說看似枯燥無味的文法概念，扭轉文法只能死背的印象，讓人驚訝文法竟然也能這麼有趣。